ACKNOWLEDGMENT

It has been a pleasure to review Mr. Danny Brewer's "Calling"; a description of one man's strife to understand how multiple life obstacles can be overcome through attention to sincere friendship, deep spiritual insight, and solid determination. While Brewer pin-points "self-teaching" as a necessary ingredient to success he also lauds the value of listening close to "mentors" along the way; and above all, reliance on a higher power in order to transcend that thin line differentiating failure and success.

David Daniels, M.A.; *Morehead State University*
(with emphasis on American Writers)

Calling

How A Man's Dream Revealed His Mission And Led Him To Truth

CALLING

HOW A MAN'S DREAM REVEALED HIS MISSION AND LED HIM TO TRUTH

DANNY BREWER
AND SUMAR SHAHIN

Published by Advantage, Charleston, South Carolina.
Member of Advantage Media Group.

Printed in the United States of America.

ISBN: 978-1-59932-204-9
LCCN: 2010905816

Most Advantage Media Group titles are available at special quantity discounts for bulk purchases for sales promotions, premiums, fundraising, and educational use. Special versions or book excerpts can also be created to fit specific needs.

For more information, please write: Special Markets, Advantage Media Group, P.O. Box 272, Charleston, SC 29402 or call 1.866.775.1696.

Visit us online at **advantagefamily**.com

PROLOGUE

In the spring of 1982, I opened my bedroom window that looked out on the porch of the five-room Kentucky farmhouse where I was raised. As I lay down and fell asleep, I saw my first cousin Delbert sitting on the porch swing. Delbert had been dead two years.

I could see him as clearly as if I were looking out the window – his square jaw and defined nose, his white hair, his round eyes. He began to tell me that I had a purpose in life. He said God had laid out a path for me if I chose to follow it.

I had met Delbert in the early 1970s, when I was fourteen and he was in his forties. He was a wealthy businessman from Florida. My parents and brother and I struggled to make a living on our dairy farm of a hundred and fifty acres, half of it wooded, near Morehead, Kentucky.

The next two nights, Delbert came to me in exactly the same way. He told me that soon I would lose two close friends. The first to go, he said, would be an older lady who not only had given me little presents but also respect and love – she showed me that I mattered as a person.

He said the second would be a man in his early thirties who helped me do repairs and odd jobs.

These were the first two people outside my family with whom I had bonded. They showed me decency and kindness. Within a couple months, both were dead: She of cancer, he in a car wreck.

Delbert also told me that I would find myself standing in a green field at a tent revival, which I would set up. I would provide the tent and seats, which I owned.

I then began to see images from my life to be. I saw a man I didn't know and knew that together we would be into something big, but I didn't know what. I understood that the man and I would be in a big auditorium doing things of this world and that after a while our journey together would be over. The man would marry and have two children, a boy and girl, and I would go on to do what I was supposed to be doing.

Later in my dream I again was in a big auditorium. A little girl about 15 to 20 years old with the sweetest face I'd ever seen stood to hand me a microphone. She had long, black hair and a dark complexion and wore a blue and white shirt. "I was in this very building before, doing things of the world," I told her, "and now I'm here doing this." I felt I was ministering.

Then the same girl was with me at the home of Delbert's widow, Alice, in Florida. We sat on kitchen stools and talked. Meanwhile, in the family room behind us to the left, Alice was speaking to seven or eight people – some family, some I'd never seen before.

I asked the girl to visit Delbert's grave with me. Alice lent me her pickup truck keys. As we were leaving, I noticed the girl's blue and white shirt had three numbers on it: 12, 26, and 27.

"What in the world are those numbers on your shirt?" I asked her. She didn't respond but gave me a weird look. At that moment I felt that the numbers were time spans.

When we reached the driveway, we saw a large tour bus, sound gear, and lighting equipment. I knew they were ours.

At the cemetery, we started down a walkway. A moss tree was to our left, and at an angle to our right was Delbert's grave. To the right of the grave was a large statue of Christ. The girl knelt at the grave to pick up a pewter-colored vase that had tipped over. I knelt beside her and reached to my left where a single yellow plastic rose lay.

As I was doing this, Delbert's spirit appeared behind us. He placed his hands on our shoulders. He asked what had taken us so long.

"It was her fault," I replied, smiling at the girl. "I was like to never find her."

The dream came to me three nights in a row exactly the same way each time.

TABLE OF CONTENTS

CHAPTER 1

On the day I was born, the doctors told my parents I wouldn't make it.

I had other ideas.

It was 1960, and my parents, Carl and Jorene, had already lost three children – two in miscarriages, and one at eighteen months old. Still, they did not lose hope even when they learned I had muscular dystrophy, which gave me a nervous condition and crippling in my arms.

Nor were they worried that medical help was not available for my condition. They had a deep faith in God, and they took me home to raise with their only other child, my brother, Hank. They kept praying, believing all would be well.

We lived on a dairy farm in a rural area of Rowan County, Kentucky, where only six homes existed until I was in my twenties. As the years passed, I continued to live at the farm and was able to help support my parents as they grew older. My brother married and moved with his family closer to Morehead.

My parents worked hard on their farm, though our home was, basically, a shack. My father helped neighbors with farm work for extra income when he could get it. We tended a garden to help keep food on the table.

When I was a little boy, two other children lived nearby, but they were not allowed to come near me. Maybe their parents believed I was contagious. Nor did other local kids want anything to do with me.

Muscular dystrophy was not something they understood. The disorder left my arms and hands very unsteady and continually shaking. I could complete many tasks, but to do so I often would need to have things brought to me. Because I was perceived as different, I was treated like an outcast, shunned and made fun of.

As early as age four, I thought it was silly for my parents to keep farming when they were not getting anywhere financially, but I didn't know what I could do to help.

Then one day I heard my father saying he had to get the oil changed in his farm tractor. Because he was not mechanically inclined, he took equipment to the shop for such work. I asked him to get the oil and I'd show him how. He thought I was crazy, but he let me show him.

"How did you know how to do that?" he asked. I told him that I just knew.

I started helping other farmers, and when I was about ten my father let me use an old smokehouse for a tool shed. I was able to make some money and felt good about being able to help my parents. I was even overhauling diesel engines.

People kept asking me how I could do such things, and I hadn't realized that not all kids my age had such ability. But I didn't believe it was a big deal. It was just so simple for me to do these things, and I couldn't understand all the fuss.

CHAPTER 2

When I went to school, the other children wouldn't sit with me in the cafeteria or pick me for their ball team. They complained if they had to sit next to me in class. They were always finding ways to make fun of me and talk about me. During a Christmas gift exchange one year, a kid who drew my name threw it back in the box. Two others did the same, until one of the teachers took my name.

When I was in second grade, a high school student tore off my coat in the middle of winter and threw it off the school bus and started laughing. I cried, not because I was embarrassed or scared but because my parents were poor and I knew they could not afford to buy me another coat.

I was humiliated daily and would come home from school bloody and in tears, begging not to have to go back. But every day, I returned. I was not scared, just embarrassed. I went through things that schools today do not allow.

I played alone, and at home I kept myself busy putting together telegraphs and anything else I could do with wire. I do not know how I was able to do these things. They just came to me, and I did them.

Even at that age, I realized I did not believe what my parents did about God. I didn't believe in God, but everyone was saying that what I was doing was a gift from him. I thought they were all silly. I saw my parents going to church regularly, helping everyone in the community they could, and constantly thanking him. For what? We cannot even buy groceries, I thought. I figured they could keep their foolish beliefs, but I knew there was no God.

I spent my first few years close to my mother and did what I could for fun. Hank was old enough to help on the farm. I watched my parents day in and day out as they farmed and gardened and helped other farmers. But I had nothing to do but play in the dirt with my toy bulldozer and ride the tractor with my dad.

The barn where they stored their tools did not have electric lighting. At age six, I was worrying that my mother might fall and hurt herself while in the barn. I asked her to get me some wire and lighting materials so I could install a light in the shed.

What an odd request, she must have thought, yet she found a way to get the materials for me. At the time the cost was very little. What my mother did not realize then was that even though I had muscular dystrophy, God had blessed me with a gift of knowledge of electricity. I successfully installed the light and switch.

That evening my father headed to the barn with a lantern to put away his tools. I caught up to him as he entered the barn.

"Dad," I told him. "You can turn on the switch to your right." He looked at me and turned it on.

"Who put the light in?" he asked. I told him I'd done it, and he looked at me in awe. My parents had no doubt that God had instilled a special gift in me.

I decided I would use my abilities to be better than all the kids who hurt me. And I wanted to start my own business with my knowledge and never be as poor as my parents. I had many talents. I welded what needed to be welded, was a plumber when needed, and did many other tasks that just came to me.

I went through school and dealt with the daily humiliation. I still did not want to be there. I watched my mom go without food to buy me shoes to be at school. My parents believed that I needed to be there as well as church, where they took me twice a week to learn how strong their faith was.

But how, I wondered, could there be a God who let this happen to me – the crippling, the rejection of my peers – when I'd done nothing to deserve it. I was smart and I could learn to take care of myself. Why did I need God?

I had a plan. I would become a master electrician and never struggle as my parents did. Heck, I'd just wired my first house. The inspector signed off on the best electrical work he had ever seen – and I was only ten years old.

One day at school in 1974, a classmate, Joey, came running to grab and pick me up. He was just having fun, but he lost his grip and dropped me. I hit the concrete steps, shattering my left knee, and was rushed to the hospital.

The doctors said they could remove the crushed pieces of my knee but did not have the technology to rebuild it. My parents and I decided against the surgery, and I wore a cast for nine months.

I was at a low in my life. The doctors had predicted I might never walk again, and I knew my parents could not afford to take me for a second opinion. A son who couldn't walk, I felt, would be a burden they couldn't bear. I had yet another reason not to believe in God. Why should I? I was already limited physically, and now this.

I never returned to school, however, and that ended the daily humiliation. I came to believe the fall had been the best thing that could have happened to me.

CHAPTER 3

This was the time my cousin Delbert and his wife, Alice, came from Florida to visit my family for about two weeks. Delbert was a wealthy and self-made businessman in his early forties at the time. Alice had long blond hair and always wore a smile. I'd heard of them for years but had never met them.

Delbert instilled in me the strength to keep fighting. He had been diagnosed with colon cancer about a year before I met him, and at that time he was given two to three years to live and had to use a colostomy bag. Delbert's strength showed me that I could get through my injuries.

Once the cast was removed, I began exercising my knee and strengthening it. Eventually, I was able to walk again. It was not a perfect walk, but I was able to get around.

I learned quite a bit about Delbert during the visit. He was outgoing and friendly but quite careful: As a wealthy man, he ran into quite a few people who used him. This did not change him internally. He had a heart of gold, never forgot where he came from, and just became wiser. I felt he was one of the most genuine, honest, wonderful people I had ever met.

The next fall, my parents and I went to Florida to visit Delbert and Alice and their family, which consisted of daughters Barbara and Joanne (and her husband, Chuck) and sons Gary (and his wife, Diane) and Dean.

Delbert made his living in the construction business, building a reputation on honesty and quality work. He had integrity and scruples unmatched.

"Praise the Lord," Delbert would say when talking with me.

Surely, I told him, he did not believe in all that.

"Absolutely," he replied. "There is a God. I do believe in him. Don't you?"

"If there is a God," I asked him, "why would someone like you be given a short time to live? And why would I be like this? I know I've never done anything to deserve all this, and after getting to know you, I know you haven't either."

He took me by the hands.

"Kid," he said, "it's not what's in your hands." He pointed to my heart, touching my chest. "It's what's right in here."

I began to think about all that had happened to me, good and bad. He started to tell me about a pastor he dearly loved, and this is what he told me next:

At his own expense, Delbert said, he had built a church in Orlando, Florida, in the early 1970s and handed the pastor the keys. The baptistery in the church was not quite completed, so Delbert offered the use of his home swimming pool for the next Sunday's baptisms. The pastor agreed.

After the sermon, as the congregation moved toward the room that housed the swimming pool, the pastor saw a billiards table in the corner. He was insulted. Playing pool, he said, was of Satan, and he left without baptizing anyone.

Delbert did not return to the church he built, nor to any other church, but he never lost his faith and belief in God. He stayed true to God in every way he could, but going to church was just not for him.

As Delbert told me this, I wondered how such a generous and decent man could be treated like that. His story did not inspire my faith. What else was this so-called God going to throw my way, and the way of my cousin and others who lived their lives decently? Where was God?

"God put you here for a reason," Delbert told me. "He has never made any mistakes. I might not know the reasons. But God will make everything good."

After our visit, Delbert kept in contact with me. Despite the miles and our difference in age, we became even closer. Four years later, he had defied the doctors: He was still alive.

CHAPTER 4

In 1979, a neighbor asked if I'd be interested in doing some electrical wiring at the sawmill where he worked. While I was there, the maintenance man quit, and I was asked to help out until he was replaced. Within a month, when it became clear I could do anything asked of me, I got the job. But I had doubts.

"Is this all I will ever be," I asked myself, "a maintenance man at the sawmill?" How could there be a God? It was just a job to me. Nothing amazing seemed to happen – until one midwinter day.

As I returned from lunch, a fellow worker yelled to me for help. He had sliced off three fingers. I didn't panic: I could feel the spirit around me telling me what to do.

I grabbed the three severed fingers and placed them in an empty cardboard box I found in his truck. Then I put snow in the box, had the man put his hand inside, packed it with still more snow, and taped the box shut.

The boss drove the man to the hospital. The doctors were able to reattach his fingers, and he soon regained almost complete use of all three. The doctors said the way I'd packed his fingers and hand had made it possible.

Another man I could not help.

It again was at lunchtime, this time on my first day of work using my trench digger at the site of Morehead State University's gymnasium addition. As a laborer high on the scaffolding unhooked his safety harness to come down, a coworker called to him to retrieve a tool that was in a dangerous place. Without his harness, the laborer went to get the tool.

I heard a loud thump behind me where he fell. He died on the spot. We read in the newspaper that he was from Tennessee, only twenty-seven, newly married. He had a little girl.

In January 1980, Delbert died. His last words were to Alice, asking her to tell me to make sure I'd come to where he was going.

We couldn't attend the funeral due to financial difficulties – not that I could have made it through anyway, because the loss left me emotionally overwhelmed. For two years after that, I went through total denial of any God, or anything supernatural. Basically, when you died, you died.

About a week after he passed, I quit at the sawmill. I was disgusted with everything. I believed that if there were a God, he would not have let someone as kind and godly as Delbert die. I hung around the house, hardly working or anything else, moping that things were just not right. And I did this for almost three years.

What was I going to do in my life? Where was I to go? What was I to do? I couldn't think straight. My mother became very worried. She took me to the doctor, and I was put on antidepressants and nerve medication.

CHAPTER 5

It was the summer of 1980, the year Delbert died, when I met Conner. At a gas station out on an old rural road, a man with blue eyes and a round face, a little overweight, approached me to ask if I knew anyone who had an old truck for sale.

I told him I had a Chevrolet truck, a '52 or '53. It had been given to me as payment for a job I did for a friend. It didn't run, but I enjoyed fiddling with it. That week, Conner came over to look at it and asked the price. I told him I'd think about it, but I knew I really didn't want to sell it.

Still, I didn't need it. And Conner wanted it. So I rigged up a tow hitch and called him to pick it up. I felt I should give it to him; I didn't want a dime for it. Months later, I learned that Conner couldn't have afforded to pay me anyway at the time, and he badly needed the truck.

We started to build a friendship. I learned that Conner played guitar and had an amazing skill: He could hear any piece once and play it, exactly the same way. Or he could revise it and make it better.

He also liked to fiddle with engines, as I did, and he would come over and teach me more about them, even diesel. Conner's knowledge of engines came from helping friends in the race car industry – he used to race one himself, a 1969 GTX Plymouth.

We became good friends, talking several times a week, and one afternoon in the summer of 1982 I told him about the dream I'd had that spring. He was the first I told. He had no doubts that my vision would come true, he later told me.

As we worked together in the barn one day weeks later, I wasn't myself. I was feeling quite down. That evening, I called Conner to thank him for praying for me.

"How did you know?" he asked.

"I just did," I explained.

He paused. "As I was leaving your place today," he said, "I had this sudden feeling that you were in need. So I stopped the car, and I prayed for you right there."

CHAPTER 6

One afternoon that same summer, I took my vehicle for an oil change to the local service station and convenience store. I could have changed the oil myself, but whenever my mother saw me use a jack to crawl underneath, she'd start screaming at me. I guess worrying about their boys getting crushed is just what moms do.

I microwaved a frozen burger, got a soda, and waited on one of the three counter stools like the ones used by Andy Griffith and his friends on the old television show.

Then I found myself floating over my body, which lay on the floor next to the stool. I could see the whole scene from all angles and wondered what was happening. I saw my body down on the floor. I saw my vehicle up on the lift.

And I could see Ray, the lanky and friendly attendant, at the pump, fueling a car. It was a gold-colored 1975 Ford LTD. He came in to get change, saw my body, yelled for somebody to call 911, and smacked me.

"Danny! Get up!" He hit me again, trying to awaken me. "What's wrong?"

I opened my eyes and looked at him. "Why are you smacking me?" He told me I had passed out and asked if I was all right.

"I saw you," I told him. "I saw everything. Like, the car at the pump."

He gave me a funny look.

"You were filling up a Ford LTD," I said, "a gold one."

"Danny," he said. "Something's not right with you."

When the oil change was done, I just left. There wasn't much more to say.

In such a rural area, you'd think the story of what happened would get around. But Ray didn't know what to think. And I was too embarrassed to tell anyone, figuring they would think me crazy and write me off. I just wanted to be part of a normal farm family. I sure didn't need more negatives.

But afterward I couldn't stop thinking about the dream I'd had that spring. I couldn't get it off my mind. Nor could I stop thinking about all that had happened to me. I began to believe the dream was crazy, illogical. Yet so many unexplainable things were happening.

In the next few months my thoughts became scattered and I grew more nervous and depressed. I felt I couldn't think straight. I felt this way for about six months, taking pills that I didn't believe in taking.

And I had lost two close friends — an older woman who lived in a nearby farmhouse whom I'd known since I was very young, and a man from Salt Lick, Kentucky, whom I'd met when he came around to help farmers with chores. Both had died just as my dream had predicted, and within two months of it.

I decided I'd had enough. I figured there was one way to get to the bottom of what the dream meant. One Friday evening, I walked into my house and told my mom I was going to visit Delbert's grave in Florida.

I believed the visit would help me come to terms with his death and understand that the dream could not be true, that it was impossible. I felt the trip would fix my state of mind. I would need only a day to see his grave, and I truly believed that it would not be as it was in the dream. That would settle all my doubts.

Throwing away all my prescription pills, I told my parents that if they wanted to join me, they should hurry and pack. My mother decided to go with me, and as she packed, she called Gary, Delbert's son, to tell him we would be heading to Florida to see him and Alice and to let him know I was going through a difficult time.

CHAPTER 7

Gary met us at his mother's house, and after greeting us, he took me aside to talk. We walked over to his father's shop, a big brick and stucco building that matched the hacienda style of the home. Delbert had loved to tinker there in his spare time.

"What kind of problems are you having?" Gary asked me. "Financial? Or did you murder someone?"

"No," I told him, not murder, and though money was always an issue, that wasn't the problem either. I said it might be spiritual, then told him about the dream.

Gary asked what his father was wearing in the dream. I described Delbert and his clothes exactly as I had seen him in the dream, and I precisely described the layout of the gravesite. Tears came to Gary's eyes.

"Would you like to see the grave?" he asked.

"Yes," I replied, and asked why he wept.

"What you described," he said, "was exactly how my father was dressed for his funeral. He looked at me intently. "And you'll see the grave for yourself."

The next morning, Gary and his wife came in their motor home and picked up my parents, his mother and I. As we approached the cemetery, I felt the urge to yell, "Stop!"

I got out and ran up the blacktop walkway, all the way to where I saw the big moss tree. Immediately to the right was the grave, and to the right of that was the statue of Jesus Christ exactly as I had seen it in the dream.

"Has that statue always been there?" I asked. Gary told me it had been placed there just a week earlier.

"Oh my God!" I exclaimed as I saw, at the bottom of the grave, a flat footstone and, in it, a vase not yet used. I knew right then that I would return someday to this grave with the girl from my dream.

As I was leaving, I looked down at Delbert's grave and told him I would be back to get him someday.

We left Florida that night and came back home. I felt blown away by what had transpired. My attitude toward the dream did a complete one-eighty, and for about a month I often sat alone, just rethinking the situation.

Gradually I returned to my daily routine. I figured I'd better get back to work, doing odd jobs that made use of my skills, because there was nothing I could do about the dream. If the numbers on the girl's shirt were spans of years, I knew I could be waiting twenty-six or twenty-seven years to see the dream fulfilled.

CHAPTER 8

One morning in 1984 I headed into town to pick up plumbing supplies for a job. As I was driving back, I saw a man putting up a tent on an empty lot. I felt drawn to him. I stopped to offer my help, which he gladly accepted. As we started to put up the tent, I noted that it looked just like the one in the dream – a basic old green tent.

He told me he was a pastor from Columbus, Ohio, who had come down to our area for a spiritual revival. He believed he was meant to be at this particular revival, even though his congregation was in Ohio. He invited me and my family to listen to his sermons every night that week. I knew my parents would enjoy the revival (much more than I would, though it sure didn't hurt me any), so we attended for two nights, including the final one.

As he finished his sermon, the pastor emphasized that it was his final night and that he must return to Ohio because his work in this area was done. He had been sent to Kentucky to minister, he said, for a sole reason: God instructed him that a certain person needed to be in contact with him and that the tent and chairs belonged to that person.

The pastor asked the group if anyone knew who that person was. I got up and told him I was that person, and I purchased the tent and chairs.

Later that summer, a couple of pastors my dad knew told him they wanted to have a revival and a pig roast and play gospel music for a week. Since we had a big open field, we decided to set the tent up there. That week my Uncle Frank, who was part of a gospel group, had revival posters made and put them up.

Over a thousand people showed up to praise God. More than fifty found salvation during that revival. About a month later, a local pastor inquired about the tent and chairs and decided to purchase them for the price I had paid.

For the next three years, nothing else related to the dream happened. I went back to my daily routine, working local jobs. I started going to church and was saved and baptized. I participated in church but still had my reservations even though by this time I believed there to be a supreme being in charge.

I still did not see any healings or miracles like the ones in the Bible – not in my local church anyway. I knew what I had seen at the gravesite. I knew what Delbert had told me. I knew what I felt. But my human side still had major doubts about the dream.

Little did I know...

CHAPTER 9

By 1987, the town had grown due to the popularity of Morehead State University. The university's new gymnasium, which took two and half years to build, had been completed several years earlier.

Rapid growth brought jobs. Roads were being widened, and we actually had a WalMart. Subdivisions and fast-food restaurants came in, including two McDonald's. Small businesses opened, and the hospital added on three floors.

In the spring of 1987, I met Dwayne, a lanky high-school sophomore from a good family. He was shy and had trouble making friends but knew right from wrong and was careful not to hook up with the wrong crowd.

He and his father, who looked like an older version of his son, had heard I had a shop and did welding and other work. They stopped to see if they could get a piece of farm machinery welded. They lived about four miles away, but I had never met them.

Despite his shyness, Dwayne took an instant liking to me – he may have felt that I, like him, was different – and he came back a couple of day's later and started hanging out.

I mentioned the possibility of converting an old truck for mud racing. I knew Conner would help since he loved working on vehicles. I soon discovered that Dwayne also had a love of vehicles. We spent our free time working together on the truck. The next spring we attended the county fair and had a ton of fun. We were both hooked.

Dwayne and I began talking about building a monster truck, a great fantasy. Little did I know that Dwayne's uncle was an executive for Ford Motor Co. Dwayne had his uncle contact the local Ford dealership to set up a sponsorship, which would make for great advertising.

The dealership did sponsor us and provided the truck, and we began to work on it. Before we knew it, Dwayne and I were appearing in several arenas, crushing cars to standing-room-only crowds. We did that for almost two years.

During that time, I also became good friends with his mother, Evelyn, and father, Dennis, a humble and God-fearing couple. They'd joke constantly about getting us girlfriends, which made Dwayne blush. It was often the topic of conversation – what is it about parents wanting to embarrass their kids?

Yet that couple was willing to help me with anything I would ever need. To this day they remain two of the best friends I've ever had.

His grandparents, Ollie and Sarah, lived next door to his parents. They were old-school, quite old-fashioned; they harked back to a slower day. I felt comfortable with them, and I knew when we met that we'd be part of one another's lives.

Whenever I came to pick up Dwayne or had something to do near their home, I'd stop to talk with Ollie and Sarah. It seemed they couldn't get enough of me, and I was amazed at the interest they took in me. Sarah was thankful to God that her grandson had met someone like me. Because I was older than his peers, she felt I would be a better influence and could bring out his less-reserved side.

She wanted Dwayne, her only grandchild, to marry and have children, but she feared she wouldn't live to see it happen because she had cancer and congestive heart failure – and because he was so shy.

That's when I began to tell her about my dream. I told her I knew he would marry, and that I had felt during the dream that she would meet the children.

I had not yet told Dwayne about my dream, however. The timing didn't seem right. We were having a great time, but I knew from the dream that our time together with our toys – the monster trucks – would be over soon.

That fall, I hinted that our fun with the trucks was coming to an end. He wondered why, so I told him then about the dream, about how he'd meet a wonderful girl, and marry, and have two children.

He naturally thought I was losing my mind. After all, he didn't even have a steady girlfriend and didn't feel at all ready to marry. But I told him he was well on his way to his destiny and that it was time for me to continue on my own path.

Our brief journey together ended. Dwayne soon married. He had two children. His grandmother lived to see them.

CHAPTER 10

After my journey with the monster trucks, I took an interest in music. My friend Conner and a guy he grew up with, Donnie, both were great guitar players, so I bought a guitar and bass to play with them. After they gave me some pointers, the playing came naturally to me, just like my knowledge of electricity.

Without taking any lessons, and despite the problem I'd had with my hands, I played bass, guitar, keyboard, and pedal steel for several local gospel groups for two or three months. My ability to play was one of God's miracles.

Other groups heard about my skill and asked me to play with them. I wanted to be a permanent member of a group, but that was not to be. Maybe it was God's will.

In the fall of 1991, a man named Malcolm who lived about four miles away called to ask about my trench digger. I met him to look at the area he needed dug up. He was tall and solid, at least 6-foot-3.

Though he was outspoken, he was extremely polite. I hadn't expected that: Others had told me he was a hardcore businessman. He offered me the job, but I still doubted he would treat me with respect. I agreed to do the work, but I felt that after that I would be done with him.

At that time I was starting to get my electrical business off the ground. I'd gotten a couple of good electrical jobs and wanted to buy a truck and more tools. I was feeling greedy, wanting money, wanting to go somewhere in my life, and I figured the electrical jobs would just be the start. I wasn't thinking about the dream.

Malcolm began to call me almost daily to ask me to look at things with him, and he'd come to the shop two to three times a week asking me to weld things and build a trailer and do other small tasks. It became petty. I felt he was absorbing the few spare minutes I had. He was getting on my nerves.

"That man has made his money and his way," I told my mother one day. "I wish that he would leave me alone. I don't have time to fool with him."

"Now, Danny, you shouldn't be like that," she said, and I felt bad. So I continued to do jobs big and small for Malcolm. He chose me to do or oversee any work he needed done. I worked for him at least six years and began to realize he was an awesome person. As my respect for him grew, I knew that he loved me.

Around the summer of 1996, as my father and I were doing some work at the home he shared with his wife, Wilma, Malcolm asked me to get down from the backhoe and talk a few minutes. We got into his truck, and he drove up behind his house.

"Son," he said, "can I ask you a favor? As long as you're here, if something happens to me will you please take care of Wilma and help her with this place?"

Absolutely, I told him. Within about three months he started to feel sick, having light seizures and headaches, and five or six months later he died of an aneurysm. And Wilma, a sweet, petite and devout woman, has become one of our family's best friends.

If I had it to do over, I would have gladly given somebody else my electrical jobs and would have called and visited Malcolm far more often. Just before we met, he had sold his business. He was bored and didn't have any true friends in the area. People just were after his money, and he knew it – but he realized early on that I wasn't like that.

Someday, I pray, God will allow me to ask Malcolm for his forgiveness.

CHAPTER 11

In 1992, I had met a girl in church who lived in a nearby town. She agreed to go out with me, but her mother slammed the door in my face when she saw me for the first time. I found out later that she told her daughter that she was not to go out with a cripple.

I wondered at the time whether I'd done something wrong, but I can see now that the incident helped me to grow. I am happy that I never ended up with that girl and am not connected with that kind of ignorance.

As I thought about my dream, I began to wonder whether there was any way it still could come true. Had too much time passed? My parents and I were growing older. We were near the age we seemed to be in the dream, and I'd had the impression they would be part of all that was to be. But their health was diminishing. I felt disheartened.

Little did I know what was about to unfold.

I couldn't sleep one night in May 1992. About midnight, I heard a voice telling me I had to build a recording studio. I could visualize it: a studio on an extended concrete slab with a work pit in it.

The voice would not stop. I thought again that I was losing my mind. Why did I need a recording studio? This was quite crazy, I thought, but then I was able to fall asleep.

On May 29, 1992, I started to pour the concrete slab. That fall, I put up the shell to the recording studio, and during the winter and early the next year I wired it and put in plumbing and some insulation. A couple of contractors gave me bids on the heating and cooling. But I ran out of money and would have to wait.

Years earlier, I'd met a man named Huey at a pallet factory where I was doing some electrical work. He was a friend of one of my schoolmates, and we struck up a conversation. He was a laid-back kind of guy with long hair – he had a hippie look about him.

After I finished my work at the factory, I lost touch with him, and I heard he'd left to pursue a career in Lexington, Kentucky. But one day about eight years after I'd last seen him, he showed up at the farm.

"I heard you were building a recording studio," he said, looking around at the work in progress. "Why haven't you finished it?"

I explained that I'd run out of money. The next day, when I got home, my mother told me Huey had stopped by again, and she asked me to put away some supplies he'd laid in front of the studio.

I went to see what was up and realized they were heating and cooling supplies. Huey hadn't mentioned that he'd become a heating and cooling contractor. I can't afford this, I thought to myself, but when Huey stopped by later and saw my concern, he told me the supplies were left over from other job sites.

In April 1993, I was on a job with my father and another employee when I had an awful feeling in the pit of my stomach. I tried to brush it off and continue to work, but it wouldn't let up. My father packed up the tools and we headed home early in the day. I was able to get into bed and fall asleep.

When I awoke about 6 p.m., I was soaked with sweat and called for my mother to take me to the hospital. I thought as we headed to the hospital in my father's truck that I just had a bad case of flu, or food poisoning, but I was hurting so bad and feeling so nauseated that I couldn't think. I couldn't get comfortable.

At the hospital, my fever was 102, and the nurse got me some Tylenol. It was just a viral infection, I was told, and it should be over in a couple of days. Hearing that made me feel better, and I was sent home.

But getting better was not to be. Not yet.

I went to bed waiting for it to pass. Three days later, I was still sick. I had no appetite, and everything I drank tasted foul. I couldn't keep any liquid down or eat. My father took me back to the hospital, where the doctors ran every test possible but still could not find a thing. They gave me antibiotics and sent me home again.

The only thing I could keep down was Gatorade and Jello, and that's what kept me alive for the next three weeks. I still hoped to get back to work soon, but as days and then weeks passed, I felt I would die.

The doctors kept changing the antibiotics. There was nothing else they could do. By now, my father had to carry me to the truck to get to the doctor. All those blood tests felt as if they were sucking me dry.

I was ill about six months, and the doctors were never able to diagnose what was wrong with me. I lost thirty-three pounds, and for a while I couldn't bear any noise or seeing anyone. But in the last few months I was able to watch some television, and I felt my body wanted to come back to me.

Little by little I started to do a few things, and finally I could get up on my own and get into the truck to visit a job site – though after watching the work a few minutes, I had to go back home to bed.

Getting sick was devastating enough, but to make matters worse I'd been hired to do a $52,000 job that was supposed to start the week after I took ill. That income would have been a great stepping stone for my family and me.

CHAPTER 12

I resumed work on the studio in the spring of 1994, buying drywall and getting quotes for installing it. I called a man named Terry who had hung some drywall for my brother years before. He stopped by at the end of his workday and asked what kind of building it was. I told him it was a recording studio.

He went back out, then returned followed by four other men. He told them to get to work, and in about forty-five minutes all the drywall was hung, with its first coat of joint compound. Terry told me they'd be back the next day to apply the second coat of mud.

I asked how much I owed him.

"You don't owe me anything, man," Terry said.

This made me feel as if the studio must be meant to be, though that was hard for me to accept even after another small miracle such as Terry's labor. I still did not understand why. What could all this be about? Why a recording studio?

The next October, a local carpet layer named Gary came by to place the carpeting on the studio walls.

"What would you need a recording studio in eastern Kentucky for?" Gary asked, and though I'd never met him before, I proceeded to tell him about my dream and that it was one of fate and not mere fantasy.

He asked for details, so I told how the visions had been coming about in my life. It had felt crazy, I told him, yet every time I'd tried to take a step away from the dream, something would stop me and it just happened – it just came together. Whether it was a friend who had materials, or who like Gary offered free labor, it just happened.

Still, the whole time I was working on the studio, I felt sick with myself and still believed I was out of my mind. There seemed to be no way to stop, though it felt Satan was at work trying to thwart my dream. I can think of no other explanation for that months-long illness that threatened my livelihood – and for another devastating blow that was soon to happen.

Meanwhile, people continued to help. One day almost two years after I'd started the project, a church friend, Betty, stopped by with her new husband, Aaron, to introduce him. She and her first husband had divorced about two years earlier.

We had a good visit. Betty is a smart country girl from a good, prayerful family. Aaron, an accomplished surgeon, seemed kind and good-spirited, and like Betty he seemed down-to-earth. Aaron asked about the studio, and I told him about the dream. The recording studio, he told me, must be God's will.

Now, Aaron on that day was still basically a stranger to me, so I felt maybe it was indeed God's will: Why else would a stranger make that comment?

To complete the studio, all I needed was to get the floor tile laid and buy the studio equipment. But there was really no rush – particularly because of finances. Aaron asked if I thought gray would be a good color for the tile. I told him that would be just fine – but again, I said, there was no rush.

I came home the next day to see an unfamiliar truck in the driveway of the studio. My mother didn't know whose it was; she'd figured I would know. I walked over and found Aaron and Betty there, almost done laying the tile. How considerate, I thought – but how could it be that a surgeon could know so much about tile work? Aaron told me that he had laid tile to put himself through school.

I asked how much I owed him. He said he couldn't take any money from me because after he'd left the previous evening, God came to him and told him to help me get the studio up and running.

Betty asked how much equipment would cost. To start, I told her, a few thousand dollars. We talked awhile longer, and they left still refusing to be paid for the materials and labor.

A few days later as I arrived home, my mother told me that Betty had come by and left me a package in the studio. Betty had told her not to let anyone into the studio until I picked up the package.

I found a large manila envelope on a table there. It was stuffed with hundred dollar bills – $10,500 worth. A note from Aaron and Betty told me to enjoy the studio. Two years after I'd started to build it, the studio soon was finished.

The following year, several groups came to record their music, and the word was out that eastern Kentucky had a recording studio. Gospel groups recorded, including one that I'd helped to start years earlier, as well as others, including rappers who sprouted at the university. Some of those who used the studio were a pleasure to work with, and some were definitely not a pleasure, but the stream of income was welcome.

As soon as he heard about it, a local real estate agent who sang Gospel came to use the studio. He was ill at the time, but I had not known that. He was on a mission to record songs involving good friends. He wanted to use the CD profits to benefit ministry work.

He needed to stay in the area for health care, however, so the recording studio enabled him to him pursue his mission. About six weeks after the CD was released, he passed away.

Every time I doubted that I was taking the right step toward my purpose, another miracle came about. How much more did I need to believe that God wanted this?

CHAPTER 13

Gary and I had become pretty good friends by January 1995, when he stopped by one day with his jeep so we could work on it in my shop. It was early on a Sunday morning when it happened.

As my father and Gary removed the gas tank, they splashed some gasoline onto the hot bulb of the trouble light they were using. The shop erupted in flames. My father and Gary were lucky to escape with their lives, but miraculously not a hair was singed on either of them. I had left the shop just before the accident to get a couple of aspirins from the house.

Everything that I owned and used for our livelihood was destroyed. Nothing was left: no tools, no truck, and no shop. I never expected anything like this to happen, so I'd never gotten insurance on my shop other than the liability coverage required by law.

At least the recording studio was untouched; it was on the other side of the property, away from the shop. But clients were few: The big thrill of having a studio in eastern Kentucky had worn off. So there was very little income, if any, from the studio. And since my illness, my electrical business still hadn't recovered.

Gary, my father and I spent two weeks cleaning up the mess, hauling the debris to the landfill. My parents and I decided then to put everything up for sale and leave as soon as Dad had what we thought would be routine surgery. We put the farm up for sale in a six-month real estate listing.

If only I could move the studio operation to Nashville, I figured, I would be able to make some good money to keep us afloat financially. As I had stood watching the shop burn, it felt like a sign to get the heck out of there. Nashville. What better place for a recording studio?

CHAPTER 14

I was in shock. Everything had finally sunk in. And my father was scared, too. Not only was he deeply worried about the loss of the family income, but he was having a biopsy for prostate cancer to see if it had spread.

Dad's younger brother had died recently of prostate cancer, and we knew the disease ran in families. This uncle lived in another state, and I scarcely knew him. But it terrified me to think that I could lose my father. The surgery was scheduled for the next morning.

At the hospital, the doctors were tied up with emergencies and couldn't get to my father's surgery until 9 that night. The doctor told us that all they would do was a biopsy, yet it was to be an overnight stay. What a joke, I thought: Hospitals should be better prepared. Dad had done without food or anything to drink for over thirty-two hours preparing for the surgery.

My father's heart stopped as he lay on the table. The doctors had not realized his level of stress when they put him under for the biopsy. After the third try with the defibrillator, an extremely weak heartbeat returned. One of the doctors told my brother that Dad had a heart attack on the table, and they decided to fly him to Lexington for further care. He lay there for thirty-one days.

After about two weeks of his hospital stay, my mother got sick. I left work to take her to the doctor. She was diagnosed with diabetes, and her kidneys were failing. She had a stress test and was told that she had major artery blockage and needed open-heart surgery immediately. But she wanted to wait until Dad's condition was stable.

At the time, my mother was caring for elderly people for extra income, and she continued to do so. Every night, we would take turns to make sure someone was with my father, not knowing which night might be his last.

On a Thursday night, as Gary and I stayed with him, my father took a turn for the worse. No beds were available in the intensive care unit, so the doctors sedated him deeply. When Gary and I finally had to leave, I believed I would never see my father alive again.

CHAPTER 15

As I sat in our truck, I said a silent prayer:

"God, I know you are real, but things were not supposed to end like this. My parents both were alive in my dreams and visions, and there are still some things that have not yet happened. Please be with my father. I could use some help here."

Gary asked if we could stop, while we were in Lexington, at the local hardware store. At the store, he saw me looking at a wrench.

"Looks like a good one for the price," he said. He asked me to put the wrench and other tools I'd chosen into the cart so he could pay for them.

"No," I said. I knew he felt guilty for the loss of my shop, but he hadn't meant to cause the fire.

A tall, lean man pushing a broom paused. He was wearing a store uniform, but no name tag – just "Edwin" penciled in on his shirt.

"Excuse me," he said. "Is your name Gary?" he asked, looking at him. How did he know?

"Your mother is in heaven," the black gentleman told Gary. He knew her name and that she'd died a few years earlier.

Then he turned to me. "God wants me to tell you that you shouldn't worry about your parents. Just tell them you love them."

The man pointed to the cart. "Those tools," he said, "are as good as the ones you just lost."

He started to walk away, then turned back to me.

"By the way, I'm not married either – just never found that special person," he said. "And your dream? It's just starting."

All the way home, neither Gary nor I could speak a word. Neither of us had ever seen this man.

When I got home, my mother asked how Dad was. I told her a white lie: He's not better, I said, but not worse. I didn't want her to worry more than necessary.

That night about 2 a.m. I heard the phone ring, but by the time I picked up the receiver, I got the dial tone. Maybe I was dreaming. The next morning, as I got ready for work, my mother told me Dad had called.

"Dad wasn't in any condition to make a call," I told her. "Are you sure you weren't dreaming?"

She saw the worry and doubts in my face and asked what was wrong.

"Can you tell me what Dad said?"

"He asked for someone to pray for him," she said, "or God was going to take him."

That day while I was doing some electrical work in Grayson, the foreman told me to return a call to my mother.

"How soon can you get home?" she asked. I braced myself for what I expected to hear next.

"Somebody needs to pick your father up at the hospital," she said. My brother and his wife had already left to get him, and by 10:30 that evening, he was home.

CHAPTER 16

While my father had been in the hospital, my friend Darryl from Nashville called. Darryl, tall and slim, worked for a company that supplied water and sewer pumps, and I'd helped install the pumps in Kentucky. We had become good friends.

"I heard you lost your shop," he said. "Are you all right? Do you plan to rebuild?"

I told him I was holding off, not knowing what would happen with my parents. I was pretty sure, though, that God had finished his work with me in eastern Kentucky. All I had left was the studio, and the studio business wasn't going well.

"I have a friend in Nashville who sells metal buildings," Darryl told me. "Do you want him to give you a call?" I told him sure, not wanting to be rude.

When Matt called a couple of days later, he asked what kind of building I wanted. I told him I wasn't really interested. But he told me he had cut a building for a customer who went bankrupt.

"I can give you a great deal on it," he said. "If those materials sit any longer, they're just going to rust. They'll go to waste."

The building, he said, measured 40 by 80 feet and was tan and brown. I was stunned by what he was telling me. Those were the precise measurements I needed, and those were the colors of my studio.

I got a loan and told him to send the building materials. They arrived in two days. As we unloaded the truck, I looked forward to having a nice-sized workshop, which I would erect next to the studio with a connecting hallway. And it would add to the farm's property value.

This building, I thought, would be my ticket out of Kentucky.

CHAPTER 17

The following Saturday, I walked out to where we were getting ready to put up the building. Gary, Huey, and another friend came to help. About 10 a.m., my father came around on his tractor and asked if we needed any gravel to be spread.

"What kind of drugs did those doctors put you on, anyway?" Gary asked him. "Can we share?" Dad's quick recovery had amazed all of us.

Then Dad began to tell us the story.

It was about 2 a.m. on a Friday morning, he told us, when he felt a shock, as if from the defibrillator, and he rose up. He could see the tangle of wires and hoses on his body. The room was very dark. He knew he was wide awake, yet he still wondered if he was dreaming.

He heard hinges creaking and a latch clicking at the foot of his bed. There he saw a big wooden door in mid-air and a spirit in a white robe. He couldn't tell if it was a man or woman. The spirit beckoned to him.

"No," he told the spirit. "Jorene and Danny need me. I don't want to leave right now." The spirit shrugged and pulled the door shut. Dad heard the door close, the hinges creak, and the latch click.

Then my father realized where he was and why he was there. He thought God must have sent an angel to take him home. He looked down at his hands and saw that he was holding down the call button.

A nurse came into the room.

"Can I help you?" she asked.

"I want to call my wife," he said. "I need to call her before I die. Would you dial the number for me?"

She did as he asked, and Mom answered the phone.

"Get someone to pray for me," he told her, "or the good Lord will take me."

"Try to get some sleep," Mom responded. "You'll be fine."

"I love you all," he said before ending the call.

The nurse looked at him.

"Carl," she said. "God sent me to pray for you. Lie down and relax and get some sleep." She laid her hands on him and started to pray.

What he felt next, Dad told us, was as if his body were zapped by a lightning bolt, rammed by an iceberg, and tossed by a tornado. He felt the hair stand up on his head.

By the next morning, he said, he felt 99 percent better. The doctor came in to check on him and was amazed by the sudden progress.

"Is there anything I can do to make you feel even better?" the doctor asked.

"Well, you could let me out of this hospital," Dad told him. "And could I talk to that little girl – the nurse who prayed for me last night? I want to thank her."

"Sure," the doctor said. He asked the nurse on duty if she knew who the night nurse had been. Dad described her: She was a black woman, and young, in her late 20s, possibly early 30s.

The nurse looked puzzled. "No nurse like that works here," she said.

CHAPTER 18

As we erected the metal building, I went over to the house to get a cooler of sodas for us. Heading back, I entered the studio and started down the hallway toward the door leading to the new shop.

"This is stupid," I was thinking. "Why am I continuing with this craziness?"

Opening the door, I froze and dropped the cooler. I slammed the door shut, unable to believe what I'd just seen. Could I be losing my mind?

I had seen a tour bus in my shop. Sitting inside was a girl who looked like the one in my dream, the girl I was yet to find, except her hair was brownish. She wore a pink, long-sleeve shirt and jeans.

Though it only seemed a split second before I slammed the shop door, I saw her come out of the bus and heard her tell me she had just loaded a couple of things onto it. On the front of the bus, I could see the letters C, H and A, and I wondered if they stood for "charter," though I knew this was hardly a charter bus.

My friends entered the studio and saw that I was shaking and white as a ghost. They wondered what was wrong, but I just asked them to please clean up my mess while I went to get another cooler of sodas.

When I returned, Gary told me he knew me too well not to see something was up. So I told them what I'd seen.

"This is making my hair stand up on my arms," Gary said. Huey gave me an odd look, one I'd never seen from him.

We entered the shop, and Gary turned on the light.

"What did you have in here?" he asked, knowing it was impossible – the doors weren't yet operating. He pointed to the concrete floor, and looking closer we saw a set of tire tracks – the size of bus tires. Gary and Huey were speechless.

The tracks remained on the concrete about two months. Quite a few friends saw them, though I never thought to take a picture.

For about four more months, the farm remained on the market. No buyers showed any interest – quite peculiar, since real estate was booming at the time and our property was prime for the location.

"God, what are you doing to me now?" I asked him one day. "How am I to find the girl in the dream if I'm stuck here?"

Most people in our part of Kentucky were white, but the girl had seemed to be of another race – so I was convinced I would have to leave the area to find her. I wanted out of there so badly that I had already started to pack boxes.

In the fall of 1995, my electrical business started to pick back up. I was able to stay busy and keep the bills paid. I picked up some new accounts, some big, some small, and bought supplies to rebuild the business.

This continued for quite a few years, but I felt disheartened: Had I done something wrong? It was as if the dream had frozen up.

CHAPTER 19

One day in 2003, I was sitting in my shop when a beaten-up Ford truck pulled up – an older model, blue and white. And out stepped Stony. He looked raggedy – was he alcoholic? Senile? His clothes were clean but worn out. I wasn't sure what to make of him, but when I shook his hand, all the odd feelings left. I felt an amazing connection with him.

After so many years, it felt to me that the dream events had just stopped. My parents were in pretty bad shape, and I was getting depressed again. I felt I was wasting my time and God's time. Maybe it was time to leave. That's when Stony and his wife moved to the neighborhood.

Over the next few years, Stony started working for me as an extra hand with the electrical work I needed to do, and he became one of my best friends. His wife, Christine, was cheerful and sweet. Her family lived in the area, and they had returned to build a relationship with her parents, who were growing older. Her parents lived in a double-wide trailer and had plenty of room but didn't invite them to stay with them, so Stony and Christine rented a trailer nearby.

Stony looked like Burt Reynolds in a cowboy hat. He had been involved in security and investigative services for the government and was a very skeptical person. We shared similar views about the economy and the state of affairs in the United States.

He was highly educated and knew his Bible, and we often talked of philosophy and biblical events and got along quite well. He was one of the most inspirational people I had met since Delbert.

"Why are you so depressed?" Stony asked me one day.

"Stony, do you have some time?" I responded. "I need to talk to you. I want to tell you about a dream I had."

First, though, I told him about my life growing up, about those feelings of not belonging, the embarrassment over my condition, the lack of faith. Then I began to tell him about the dream. He didn't say a word.

"I'm going to be like Paul Harvey," I told him, "and give you the rest of the story."

He laughed. "You mean there's more?"

I related then all that had happened that I felt was part of the dream coming to pass. But for the last few years, I added, the dream had seemed to be frozen in time, and it felt more and more as if I didn't belong there.

"Maybe God froze the dream because I didn't at first believe in him," I said. "I was actually very mad at him after all the things that happened. It seemed the closer God wanted me to get to him, the more I hated him."

Hate is a strong word, but I didn't know how else to describe a feeling that was close to hatred but not quite. I hadn't known I could feel hatred of anyone, let alone God. Maybe a better word would have been rage – rage over the pain I was feeling – or just plain hurt.

As we talked, we walked toward the shop and recording studio. Stony was wondering about my sanity, I found out later. He hadn't pegged me for a loony. But when he realized that I was actually collecting equipment as I was describing in my vision, he listened intently.

He asked for details and a description of the girl, which I gave him. I told him about her shirt with the numbers and said she had the voice of an angel, clear as a bell. Stony was quite in awe.

We sat down. "I don't think you hate God," he said. "I believe you are hurt."

Then he related the story of Job as it was never told to me before. I'd read the story, of course, and heard it preached, but never with such intensity. I truly understood it for the first time. He made me feel the story, not just know it. In a calm and still manner, Stony told each heartbreaking detail of the many travails that Job endured.

"It's like what you are going through in your life," Stony said, looking at me.

As time went on, Stony talked to my friends with whom I'd shared the dream. In the Bible, he knew, a true vision continues to grow – it does not fade away to be forgotten as a common dream does. I found out later that Stony was trying to find out about me, basically investigating me and my claims.

He asked one friend, a self-made businessman well known in the area, what he thought of my dream. My friend told Stony that I was intelligent, trustworthy and reliable and that I'd given him the exact same account of it. Hearing that from a man of such caliber helped to validate my story for Stony.

Stony stopped by the shop one day and asked if we might pray together right away.

"I would be happy to," I replied. I'd been telling him that I could not, in all good conscience, pray to God about the vision, and Stony knew I didn't mean that.

We prayed intensely. We prayed for my vision to be completed and for me to find the girl. We also prayed for family and friends and enemies alike. We truly felt blessed in our prayer. Stony believes he has been blessed by my friendship and the knowledge that God is working through me.

When he left, in October 2008, I called a real estate agent to appraise my property. It was time to go to Nashville.

Three nights later, when the appraiser was to meet me, I had to cancel the appointment. My mother was having chest pains, and we were off to the hospital. I threw up my hands: "Here we go again. God, why?"

It was as if I was being stopped every time I wanted to leave to pursue the dream.

CHAPTER 20

Two to three weeks later the local truck stop, which had been closed about two years, reopened. I was accustomed to doing business in town at the Marathon station, and though the truck stop was closer, I continued to go into town. I had no intention of frequenting the truck stop, particularly since it didn't accept checks.

One morning my mother suggested I try the breakfast at the truck stop's diner, since she wasn't feeling well and couldn't cook that morning. I enjoyed it, and I can be quite picky. So a couple of weeks later my employee and I decided to stop for dinner there.

The owner, Sam, noticed my work truck and asked to borrow a hacksaw. A tall man with a dark complexion and big brown eyes, he was polite and seemed genuine. He returned a few minutes later and asked if I'd help him install an ice machine. I agreed, and the store manager came by.

"Great, we have help," she commented. Another foreigner, I thought.

Sam and I started talking, and I asked if he'd have any problem accepting my checks since that's how I kept records for my electrical business.

"I don't have a problem with that at all," he said.

As I pulled out of the parking lot, I thought about the store manager. There was something about that lady.

A couple of days later, I stopped into the truck stop and bought a soda. I saw the store manager, and looked at her name tag.

"Is that your name – Sumar?" I asked. "Like, summer?"

"Yes it is."

"I like that. That sure is a pretty name."

Something about her made me feel that I had to get to know her, and I wasn't sure why. She wasn't quite short, but definitely not tall. Her large, brown eyes were honest, and she struck me as a genuine person.

I wasn't sure whether she was Sam's wife or a member of the family. I learned later that she and her son, AJ, worked for Sam. I wondered where she came from. I'd had some run-ins with foreigners but felt she was a good person.

I began frequenting the truck stop, enjoying the friendly atmosphere. About a month later when I stopped in to get a soda, Sumar was sitting in front of the tobacco display, rearranging and dusting. She got up to ask me a question. We started to talk, and AJ, who was behind the counter, joined the conversation.

Sumar began talking about the challenge of making the truck stop a success.

"It's really odd," she said, "that I ended up in eastern Kentucky. I don't know why God brought me here."

She told me that she was a city girl, born in Chicago into a family from a strong, traditional Palestinian culture. When she married, she moved to a suburb of Detroit in Wayne County, Michigan, where her husband, Alex, was from. They lived there for twelve and a half years. Their three children were born there.

Then Alex and she decided to move to Lexington, where she had family. Sumar told me that her background was in management and she was asked to get the truck stop off the ground. She said that she loved challenges but never had managed a business that big and diverse.

While she was wondering why God brought her to eastern Kentucky, I told her I was wondering why God was keeping me in eastern Kentucky.

"Why?" she asked. "What has God done to you?"

I told her that if she had a few minutes, I would give her some highlights. And I began to do so, as she and AJ listened in awe.

"Now I know why I ended up here," she said. "To meet you, Danny, and hear your story so it can remind me that God still existed."

I wondered why she felt that way about God. I learned later that she had stopped going to church and had been feeling numb since the illness and death of a sister she dearly loved. To be with her sister was part of the reason she had moved to Lexington.

I started to tell them about the studio – a fun hobby, I said, though I didn't say it was part of my vision. Sumar told me about her daughter having a beautiful voice.

"Aw, Mom," said AJ, "you're just biased, she can't sing." After a few funny exchanges between mother and son, our conversation ended. Sumar had to get back to work.

A couple of days later, one of Sumar's daughters, Lynn, was behind the counter when I paid my lunch bill. I asked if she was the daughter who could sing. She said she could but that she was too shy to do so in front of anybody.

"I do have a little sister," she added, "whose voice is better than mine. I'll bring her to the truck stop so you can meet her."

CHAPTER 21

My cousin-in-law, Clifford, called me in the middle of the following week. Clifford lives in Florida, and the call was quite odd because he generally would call on a Sunday afternoon.

He told me some very special people were coming into my life and I should be very good to them despite my preconceived impression. He didn't know who they were, but they were somehow connected to my vision.

In the middle of May 2009, I walked into the truck stop to grab a soda. Sumar stopped me so I could meet her other daughter, 17-year-old Chandler, who had come up from Lexington.

Sumar noticed I was driving my Chevy Avalanche, rather than my work truck, and asked if I liked it. It was her and Chandler's favorite model of truck, she said. As I was offering Sumar the keys to take it for a test drive, Chandler came around the corner, smiled, and asked if she could drive it instead.

Sumar was worried because her daughter was a new driver, but off Chandler went. She returned safely and said she'd loved it.

"Can I have it?" she asked, smiling. I just said maybe one day.

During the next couple of months, I continued to do work around the truck stop. Sumar told me it was a blessing that I was always around when needed. She and I became good friends and often talked about the dream.

That August, the truck stop sponsored a benefit motorcycle show for a local person in need. I provided the stage, tents, chairs and equipment. Sumar asked me to sit with her, her husband and daughter. She wanted me to tell Alex about the dream.

Alex is a polite and kind man with a round, dark face and glasses. I gave him some highlights and told him I'd go into detail when we had time. While I was talking to him, his face lit up.

"I believe this is why God put me here," Sumar said, looking at his wife. "God does things that we don't understand, Sumar."

That surprised me. I had wondered if he'd think I was the strangest person he'd ever come across and tell me not to speak to his wife again.

Three days later, Alex and Chandler came back up from Lexington. Chandler had overheard the highlights of the dream and asked to speak to me. She wanted to hear more about it.

Her parents and I sat in the diner and I started to go into more detail. When Sumar and Alex got to talking about something else, Chandler asked them to stop so she could listen. Her parents moved to another table to finish their conversation.

Chandler asked me to describe the girl in the dream.

"It's kind of strange," I said, "but the little girl looks exactly like you, dark complexion, big eyes, and petite, except her hair is black."

Chandler laughed. "Danny, my hair is black. I just dye it."

I told her I felt that very soon I would be meeting the girl, or had already met her and didn't know it. In a short time, I said, things would happen that had to do with the number 27 that I saw on the girl's shirt – and it was that number I thought about, not the other two. I've yet to know the meaning of the other two.

I didn't suspect that Chandler might be the girl in the dream. I told her I had to leave to take care of a few things. As I left, I wondered if I'd weirded her out and would never see her again.

CHAPTER 22

Sumar had always believed that Chandler could sing. But she never thought her dream for Chandler to become a singer would come true – she and Alex didn't have the connections or finances to provide her with music lessons or studio time.

Chandler was shy when it came to music, though friendly and outspoken otherwise. If she could see my studio, Sumar believed, she might overcome her shyness and have an opportunity for others to hear her gift.

Chandler put up a fuss, believing that her mother had ulterior motives for wanting her to see my studio. Sumar assured Chandler that she wouldn't have to sing. Sumar later told me that she believed that once Chandler saw the studio, she would naturally want to sing. Sumar believed God had given Chandler a gift and it was to be used.

That following Saturday, Sumar was at the truck stop and she let me know that she was getting ready to leave early. That was unusual for Sumar. I asked what was up.

"I'm headed into Lexington for the weekend," she said, "to celebrate my twenty-seventh wedding anniversary."

I was blown away. Twenty-seven. I told her to have fun, and as I was leaving, I asked God: "Please, don't. Just don't. This cannot possibly be. Do not let me get entangled with these people."

I never wanted to see Chandler again. I was terrified. I had expected that the girl who was supposed to be in the ministry with me might be from a Third World country, maybe an orphan. I never thought she would have such strong family ties and cultural roots.

But I also thought that she must be the girl in my dream – and that Sumar and Alex, no matter how much they believed in the truth of my story, would never accept that Chandler was that girl.

CHAPTER 23

Two weeks later, Sumar asked me if I would be home on Saturday so that she, Alex and Chandler could see the studio. When Chandler walked into the studio and sat down in the control room, she smiled a smile that none of us will ever forget. Without a word from any of us, she ran out to her car to get her music.

It felt as if Sumar's dream for Chandler would come true. I told her that any time Chandler wanted to come to sing, she was surely welcome. They were appreciative but didn't want to impose, knowing that studio time was expensive. Sumar and Alex asked me about price. I told her the studio was available to Chandler at no cost. I just felt that it was the right thing to do.

The three of them asked to see the whole studio. They walked down the hallway to where I had spilled the soda, and as they opened the door I realized that Chandler looked exactly as the girl in my vision there had appeared – the same T-shirt and jeans, the same hair color.

And it struck me that the letters I'd seen that day on the front of the bus, C-H-A, did not stand for charter, as I'd imagined. They stood for Chandler!

Chandler went into the studio to sing. As I set up the equipment, I felt as strange as I'd felt back in 1995 when I met the man pushing the broom in the Lexington hardware store. I knew Chandler belonged in the studio. It was hers.

I knew Sumar was happy that Chandler decided to come, but I don't think she realized that her daughter was the girl in my dream that I'd told her about. When Chandler started singing, Sumar looked for my reaction.

"Danny, what do you think, honestly?"

"The little girl needs work," I said, "but she has potential to be awesome, if she gets over her shyness." I felt that she had a good disposition and that something about her would make her a big star.

Like his wife, Alex was amazed that eastern Kentucky had a recording studio and that their daughter was there singing in it. He told Chandler that she'd better take advantage of the opportunity and practice. He knew she had talent, and it was clear he was proud of her.

"She has a naturally awesome voice," I told them.

I was thinking she had the voice of an angel.

EPILOGUE

As I write this, Chandler is spending at least one day every week practicing in my recording studio. Sumar and Alex bring their daughter from Lexington, together when they can. Sometimes Lynn comes, too, and sings with her sister; she, too, has a lovely voice.

This family and I have become wonderful friends. I am amazed that these people have come into my life. I couldn't have picked more genuine friends, and they feel blessed for knowing me.

Chandler is adjusting to the fact that she has access to the miracle of music. Overwhelmed by the knowledge she could have an amazing future, she is not rushing. She is in her last year of high school and doing her best to enjoy every minute. None of us is pushing her. We are letting her practice at her pace and enjoy herself.

Sumar no longer manages the truck stop – Sam sold his share in it – but she still drives to eastern Kentucky at least once a week with Chandler so that the opportunity is not lost.

I do not know if Chandler realizes that I truly believe this studio was built for her. When I reflect on the vision of the studio, and when Sumar and I speak of it, we believe it was meant to be.

You see, Chandler was born at the end of May 1992. This is around the time that I had the vision for the recording studio. At the time, Sumar told me, she never expected she could get pregnant again, due to previous difficulties and a miscarriage. Chandler came as a total surprise.

God recently showed me yet again that he has something for us all to do. Dad and I took my mother to Lexington for a check-up. At the doctor's office, he was helping her down a hallway with her walker. As I walked in front of them, my cell phone rang. I muted it.

Then I heard Mom say she felt weak. "Catch me, I'm going to fall," she said, and as I turned, I heard a thump. She and Dad both were on the floor: He had tried to soften her fall.

My mother was not breathing. I tried to get her to respond. She would not. I ran to the nearest office and asked them to call 9-1-1. A nurse came from the office and immediately started to try to revive Mom, who had no pulse.

When the EMTs arrived, they pulled out a defibrillator and heart monitor, but the equipment wouldn't work. They checked her again, and one EMT turned to the other: "She is gone."

They called for a gurney, and as they picked her up, Mom's eyes opened. "What are you all doing to me?" she asked. At that moment, my cell phone rang again, and once again I muted it.

They took her to the emergency room in the hospital across the street, and I went to the waiting area. My father had looked stunned after the fall, but he hadn't been injured, and he wouldn't leave his wife.

I decided to calm down and check my cell phone. I saw the times those two missed calls had come in. They were about fifteen minutes apart – from the time Mom fell to when she opened her eyes. I know that for at least twelve of those minutes, probably longer, she lay on the floor without breathing, her heart still.

Since I was in Lexington where Sumar lived, I gave her a call, and she came to the hospital. As we waited in Mom's room for her to get a CAT scan, I told Sumar the details of what had happened. Mom was then wheeled in. She chatted with Sumar and asked her how Chandler was doing.

Later, Sumar commented that my mother could not possibly have been dead, not even for ten minutes with no oxygen to the brain, and awake to have a conversation afterward.

"God was definitely at work," she said. "He definitely wants her to be alive – to see our project through." And God, I know, wants to see us all through. He knows his plan for every one of us.

As a young man, I had a dream of things yet to be, and though at times in my life that vision has felt like a curse, I know now that it was a blessing. God has shown me how his long and loving arms bring people together to fulfill his master plan. He touches and directs our lives.

I have come to understand that I always must do what God wants me to do, no matter what happens. As I write this, I have yet to see how the visions he sent to me will ultimately play out, but I felt compelled to share my story, even as it unfolds, to encourage others to trust in him.

I dream, now, of giving back to God more and more of my time and whatever talents he has seen fit to give me. He is with us, and he truly is in charge of our lives – if we allow him to be.

SUMAR'S STORY

I was born in September 1962 in Chicago, Illinois, my parents' second child. Their first was my brother, born thirteen months earlier. My mother was from a big family, but my father was an only child, raised by his mother. Both are from the Middle East and grew up in traditional Orthodox Christian families. Though my father was born in the Middle East, he is an American citizen because my grandfather fought for the United States in World War II.

My grandfather died before my father was born, however. He was building a house for his new family, and while digging a well he got pneumonia. My grandmother refused to remarry, concerned that her son would not be treated properly if she did. But she herself locked him in a closet sometimes when she had to go to work and no one was around to care for him.

As my father became older, he frequently thought of coming to America so that he could make a living and be able to support his mother. This way he could take care of her and she could stay home. He felt it was his obligation and he would be able to make a better life for both of them.

When he turned seventeen, he boarded a ship and was on his way. He went first to Pittsburgh, briefly, then lived several years in Detroit, and eventually moved to Chicago when an uncle asked him to open a restaurant with him.

He had learned proper English but had trouble, when he arrived, understanding how Americans talked. He took words literally. If someone told him, "See you later," he would wait hours expecting their return, so as not to be rude. When he found work, he sometimes got into fistfights with coworkers when he took their slang literally and felt insulted. As time went on, his understanding improved, yet he still believed that people should use proper English since it was a good language. Slang felt quite disrespectful.

My father worked until he was twenty-eight years old, when he decided to go back to the Middle East and try to find a wife. The year was 1960. He had already sent for his mother and set up a home. Now he wanted to share his life with a woman, one who would bear him children – sixteen, maybe – and who would be good company for his mother.

Upon his return to the Middle East, he spotted the girl who would become my mother. She was leaving school one day, and he tried to stop her. Not knowing him, my mother ran home, but my father followed and found out who she was.

He went to his aunt's house to tell her about the girl he'd seen. His extended family got together and, following tradition, contacted the girl's family. The elders planned a visit. My mother was asked to make coffee and bring it out to my father's family. She did. That was how it went. They were engaged, and they married within a week. She was the second born in her family and the first of her siblings to be married, just as I was.

Ten days later, my mother, at age nineteen, left for America with a man she barely knew. That was the way of our culture. She did not yet have any family in the United States, and she was going to be living with a man and woman she didn't know. Yet my parents grew so completely in love that they could believe their way of meeting and marrying was how it should always be done.

My brother was born in 1961, and my parents were happy. It was always good to have sons. By 1967, they had four daughters. They both wanted a brother for their eldest, and my mother felt my father would be upset. But my father just told her that if the girls were healthy and kept looking like her, she could give him as many girls as she wanted. That was quite an unusual attitude for a Middle Eastern man.

We were disciplined in a way that is now known as child abuse. That was the way my father and many parents of his generation thought was proper. They basically did not know any other way. We were actually chained to stairs.

My older brother and I were the ones who received the most abuse. Because we were the oldest, our parents believed that if we were disciplined correctly, the other children would follow our footsteps and not need as much. My older brother resented my father for it, but I always understood that what my parents did to us was out of love and without malice. I even joke about it today when I say, "I was abused with the most love any child could ever have."

When I was four years old, we moved from our little house to a bigger one. My mother was pregnant with her fifth child, and we needed the space. We still lived in the city, but closer to the suburbs. The neighborhood seemed pretty nice. Little did we know.

Because of our darker complexion, we were all treated cruelly. When my brother and I started school, we were called names, made fun of, and treated meanly in a way that would not be allowed today. We went through this treatment day in and day out. My parents tried to help us understand.

I suppose I just accepted it. What people did and said could hurt badly, and even at that young age I knew that things did not have to be as they were, that people could act better. But there was nothing I could do about it.

My older brother had a very difficult time with it, however. He wanted friends. Playing with his sisters was getting old. But so that he could have some friends, my brother picked the wrong ones. He led us on a path that we did not want to be on.

I buried my pain in schoolwork and excelled so I could feel worthy and good about myself. My brother got more of my parent's attention than I did because they felt he needed it. My parents felt I had a deeper understanding about our situation and that I did not need as much guidance.

I loved my brother dearly, but I also became close with my sister Amanda who was old enough to tag along with me around the house. She was a tough cookie. As we got older and she started noticing how we were being treated, she would have none of it. She had no problem telling anyone what she thought. She beat every boy who arm wrestled her. They were not going to mess with her.

I was too soft to want to hurt anyone. I felt if I ever instigated a fight, I would lose. I had never fought anyone, not even my siblings, so if anyone bothered me, my older brother would stop them. But a girl in my class kept telling me to meet her after school so we could fight, just because she felt like it. I kept telling her to leave me alone, and I would walk a different route home every day to avoid her. One day she caught up with me in an alley. I built up my confidence, said a small prayer, and started punching her until she was on the ground. She never bothered me again.

Amanda, who was two years younger than me, was always the closest to me. We were totally different. I was a totally old soul as far as seeing things beyond my years and understanding situations around me, when children my age couldn't or shouldn't. But she should have been born in the 1800s. She was just so old-fashioned.

My father and I were also very close. These two were the only ones who completely understood me as a person in my family. We were able to discuss anything; whether we agreed or not, we understood the other's viewpoint.

This brought on a lot of unconventional conversations between my father and me – things that my mother thought girls should not discuss. Boys were allowed basically to discuss and do just about anything, whereas girls had to always be ladylike. But even if I debated until I turned blue, and even if my father agreed with me, as he often did, I was not going to change our culture. We would still be who we were.

This posed problems for me when I got older because I wanted to travel and get a good education. My father had no problems with that, as long as I got married. Our culture required that I could not do these things unless I had a man. I did not agree, but I could not sway from the culture.

By the time I was nineteen, I had married Alex and moved to a suburb of Detroit, where he was from. In our culture, the man comes to the girl's hometown to marry, but she then goes with him to his town. By age twenty-one, I had my first child, AJ. My father called me: Now that I was married and had a son, he said, "go back to school." When my son turned a year old, I did as he suggested.

When I graduated from business school, wages were not high enough to make my working worthwhile once we paid for child care. Alex could support the family – he and his father owned an office supply company – so I decided to stay home and try to have more children.

Coming from a big family, I had always wanted four children: two boys and two girls. I know I was blessed to have sisters and brothers. I believed I could plan everything. But that was not to be. After two years I still was not pregnant.

My father passed away when I was twenty-four. That was one of the most devastating things that has ever happened to me. But then I became pregnant with Lynn. She was a complete surprise and blessing. Shortly after her birth, I became pregnant again but miscarried.

At times I felt that God was smacking me to understand that things would be his way, not mine. Of course there were always ups and downs in my life, and our marriage also had its ups and downs. But we kept on going. We never believed in divorce and did not want a broken home for our kids.

I didn't think I would get pregnant again, but four years after Lynn was born, along came Chandler. I felt bad that AJ did not have a brother yet, but I prayed for another girl. Things at this point in my life were quite difficult. Somehow, I figured a girl would handle things better if Alex and I split.

A few months before Chandler was conceived, I told my husband I thought we should move from Michigan, hoping things would get better. When I found out I was pregnant, it certainly felt that God again was showing that he would do things his way, not mine, and that it was not time to leave Michigan.

Nevertheless, I told Alex that when Chandler was one year old, I was moving whether he came with me or not. I knew he didn't like Chicago but suggested he work on his resume: I would go anywhere he wanted. When a year had gone by, I reminded him of our conversation. Though he had prepared his resume, he had not taken any other initiative.

We discussed different places, and Alex did not have any preferences other than not moving to Chicago. So I suggested we move to Kentucky so I could be near other family members who had moved there from Chicago approximately a year and a half earlier. I'd been away from them for twelve and half years.

Alex did not have a problem with moving there, so I enlisted my sister in house hunting for me. On July 1, 1993, we moved to Lexington. Alex did not follow right away because he had to finish some business dealings. At the time, I was waiting tables and was able to transfer. My family helped me care for the children while I worked. I only took employment that would allow either Alex or me to watch the kids.

We spent a lot of time with my family, and I was especially thankful that I could be with my mother and sisters. Amanda had become very ill and she was deteriorating. I was able to spend her last years with her. I feel blessed for that. I even thought that might be the reason I ended up coming to Lexington.

Still, I felt numb. I couldn't attend church anymore. I felt totally betrayed by God. My sister's children were young at the time. All of my nieces and nephews as well as my children were very close to her. I didn't cry so much as I just went through my life without really enjoying anything or believing anything could be right. My mother did not deserve to lose a child, and I didn't deserve to lose the only other person in my life with whom I felt a total connection.

Or maybe I did deserve it. Had I done something wrong? I felt my whole life had been doing everything to be the best daughter, wife, and mother that I could for my whole family, and of course I didn't regret that. Did God want more from me? Maybe my life was not supposed to be about me.

Perhaps I was being ungrateful, I thought; after all, I had a husband and three healthy and beautiful children. What more could I ask? I know I am blessed, and I am grateful, but there are times I think of so many things I would like to do. Will I ever get to do what I have dreamed about? Maybe, or maybe not.

These past few years have been a roller-coaster for me, and I have accomplished some good things. One was the opportunity to build a business from the ground up and to be recognized not just as a good-looking woman but also as an intelligent one.

I got that opportunity after meeting Sam, who noticed my business sense and determination. Within a few years he became my boss at the truck stop, where I met Danny.

I hadn't known anyone in the community where the truck stop was located – whom to trust to do repairs or answer questions about the area. Danny could help with anything. I felt bad for calling him to do so much work, but whether the job was big or small, he was polite and never treated me like an idiot.

Danny assured me he was always happy to help. He was interesting, I thought when I met him. As time went on, I came to believe he was a guardian angel.

Advantage Media Group is proud to be a part of the Tree Neutral™ program. Tree Neutral offsets the number of trees consumed in the production and printing of this book by taking proactive steps such as planting trees in direct proportion to the number of trees used to print books. To learn more about Tree Neutral, please visit **www.treeneutral.com.** To learn more about Advantage Media Group's commitment to being a responsible steward of the environment, please visit **www.advantagefamily.com/green**

CALLING is available in bulk quantities at special discounts for corporate, institutional, and educational purposes. To learn more about the special programs Advantage Media Group offers, please visit **www.KaizenUniversity.com** or call 1.866.775.1696.

Advantage Media Group is a leading publisher of business, motivation, and self-help authors. Do you have a manuscript or book idea that you would like to have considered for publication? Please visit **www.amgbook.com**

www.ingramcontent.com/pod-product-compliance
Lightning Source LLC
La Vergne TN
LVHW020649100826
845148LV00012B/2398

* 9 7 8 1 5 9 9 3 2 2 0 4 9 *